HAUNTED
Dolls

Martha London

raintree

a Capstone company — publishers for children

Raintree is an imprint of Capstone Global Library Limited, a company incorporated in England and Wales having its registered office at 264 Banbury Road, Oxford, OX2 7DY – Registered company number: 6695582

www.raintree.co.uk
myorders@raintree.co.uk

Edited by Maddie Spalding
Designed by Becky Daum
Production by Colleen McLaren
Printed and bound in India

ISBN 978 1 4747 7360 7
22 21 20 19 18
10 9 8 7 6 5 4 3 2 1

Acknowledgments
iStockphoto: alex_black, 26–27, AlpamayoPhoto, 14–15, tobkatrina, 23, TugbaKibar, 8–9; Newscom: Ellen Creager/Detroit Free Press/MCT, 19; Shutterstock Images: Eldar Nurkovic, 5, GIO_LE, 17, 30–31, John Arehart, 20–21, Maria Dryfhout, 11, 28, Perfect Lazybones, 24–25, Prachaya Roekdeethaweesab, 6–7, Shchus, cover, Sorah Malka Rosenberg, 12–13
Design Elements: iStockphoto, Red Line Editorial, and Shutterstock Images

CONTENTS

CHAPTER 1

EVIL
Dolls

It is night time. You are in your bedroom. Moonlight shines in from your window. You notice movement. A doll sits on your windowsill. Did it move? Its glass eyes stare back at you. Could it be watching you?

Dolls may look scarier at night than they do during the day.

Some people think dolls can become **haunted**. They say dolls can be **cursed**. They believe people can put spells on dolls. The spells make the dolls move.

Some people think dolls can be cursed or haunted.

Some people also think **spirits** can haunt dolls. The spirits are said to control the dolls. They make the dolls do evil things.

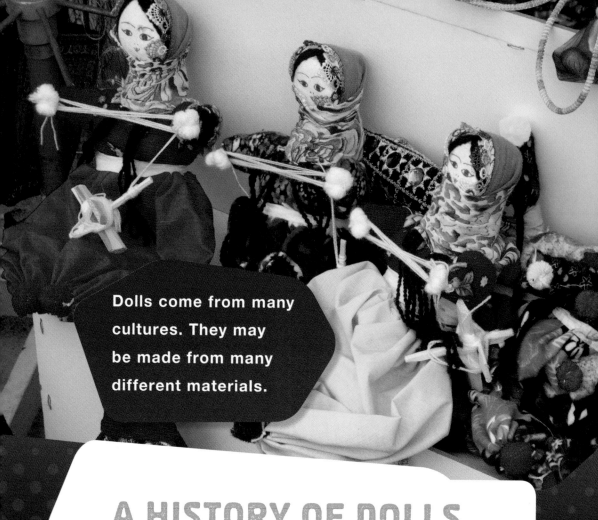

Dolls come from many cultures. They may be made from many different materials.

A HISTORY OF DOLLS

Dolls have been around for thousands of years. Most dolls today are toys. But dolls were not always used as toys. Some were gifts to gods. The gifts were meant to bring the giver good luck.

Some **ancient cultures** didn't let children play with dolls. They thought dolls were dangerous. They believed dolls held powerful magic.

STONE DOLLS

In 2004 a doll was found on an island near Italy. It was carved out of stone. It was 4,000 years old!

CHAPTER 2

ANNABELLE

Imagine a doll with big black eyes. The doll is made of fabric. It has red wool for hair. It has a smile like a scarecrow. You can find a doll like this at a museum in Connecticut, USA. The doll's name is Annabelle.

Annabelle is a Raggedy Ann doll. Raggedy Ann dolls became popular in the early 1900s.

Annabelle is a doll from the 1970s. Annabelle was a gift for a woman named Donna. Donna kept the doll in her apartment. Then she began to notice strange things. She would leave the doll in one room. But the doll would appear later in a different room. Donna sometimes found the doll on her bed. The doll was often in a different position from the way she had left it. Sometimes it was upright. Sometimes it had its legs crossed.

Raggedy Ann dolls are stuffed with cotton. But their legs and arms can be moved.

Some dolls are thought to be controlled by the spirits of dead people.

BRING IN THE EXPERTS

Donna called a **medium**. Mediums believe they can communicate with spirits. The medium said the doll was haunted. She said a girl's spirit controlled the doll. The girl's name was Annabelle Higgins. Annabelle was a real person. She had died many years earlier.

The medium said Annabelle's spirit was not mean. So Donna kept the doll. But things got worse. Donna's friend was in her apartment one night. He woke up with scratches on him. He said Annabelle had attacked him.

ANNABELLE

The 2014 film *Annabelle* is based on the Annabelle doll's story.

The doll in the 2014 film *Annabelle* looks different from the original Annabelle doll.

Annabelle was moved to a museum. Today Annabelle sits behind a glass case. The case is always locked. A sign warns visitors: "Positively Do Not Open."

CHAPTER 3

ROBERT

Robert is more than 100 years old. He is 90 centimetres (3 feet) tall. He wears a sailor suit. Robert looks like a boy. But he is a doll. His eyes are made of buttons. His body is made of wood.

A boy named Gene got Robert as a gift in 1904. Gene talked to Robert at night. Gene's parents heard two voices coming from the room. They sometimes heard a giggle. The giggle didn't sound like it came from Gene.

Robert is on display at a museum in Key West, Florida, USA.

Old dolls may be put in glass cases to keep them in good condition.

STRANGE EVENTS

Gene grew up and got married. He kept Robert in the attic of his house. Children who lived nearby often avoided the house. They said they saw Robert move in the attic windows. They claimed he moved from window to window.

Today Robert is in a museum in Florida. He sits in a glass case. Some visitors say they've seen him move.

HIDING ROBERT

Gene's wife didn't like Robert. She hid Robert in a trunk after Gene died.

CHAPTER 4

MANDY

Some dolls look like babies. They have round cheeks. They have lifelike eyes. A doll named Mandy looks like this. She wears a nightgown. She was made in the early 1900s. Some people say she is haunted.

Dolls that look like babies became popular in the early 1900s.

A woman once owned Mandy. She kept Mandy in her cellar. She sometimes heard crying from the cellar. She believed the sounds came from Mandy. She didn't want Mandy in her house any longer. She gave Mandy to a museum in Canada. She said the crying stopped once Mandy was gone.

Some dolls have glass eyes that move. It may feel as if they're watching you!

CAMERA PROBLEMS

One visitor tried to film Mandy. But her camera kept turning on and off.

MUSEUM HAUNTINGS

Mandy was put inside a glass case. People noticed strange things after Mandy arrived. Museum workers said their lunches kept disappearing. Their lunches turned up later in drawers. Some visitors say Mandy's eyes follow them. Others say they've seen Mandy blink.

Strange events have sometimes been reported around dolls. Some people say this is because dolls are cursed or haunted. What do you think?

GLOSSARY

ancient
old or occurring in the past

culture
a group that has its own beliefs and traditions

cursed
something that is believed to be controlled by a spell

haunted
having mysterious events happen often, possibly due to spirits or cursed objects

medium
a person who is said to communicate with spirits

spirit
a ghost or supernatural being

TRIVIA

1. Dolls can be made of many materials. Dolls in ancient Egypt were made of clay and wood. Dolls in ancient Greece and Rome were made of stone. Today many dolls are made of fabric or plastic.

2. Haunted dolls have been the subject of many movies. Since the 1970s more than 40 films have been made about haunted dolls.

3. The doll Annabelle is housed in the Warren's Occult Museum in the USA. Ed and Lorraine Warren opened this museum in 1953. They also investigated reported hauntings. The couple reportedly investigated more than 10,000 hauntings.

ACTIVITY

Come up with your own spooky haunted doll story. Get creative! Look back through the stories in this book. What are some common events or occurrences you notice? How might you use these in your own story?

Tell your story to your friends or family. You might find a dark place to tell it. This may make your story seem spookier. Watch how your audience reacts. Did you get the reaction you were hoping for? If not, how might you make your story scarier?

What would the doll look like in your haunted doll story?

FIND OUT MORE

Books

Dolls of Doom: A Tale of Terror, Michael Dahl (Raintree, 2018)

Paranormal Handbook to Ghosts, Poltergeists and Haunted Houses, Sean McCollum (Raintree, 2016)

True Stories of Ghosts, Paul Dowswell (Usborne, 2012)

Websites

A 'haunted Britain' interactive map:
www.visitbritain.com/gb/en/haunted-britain-explore-our-map

Discover scary stories from history:
www.dkfindout.com/uk/explore/real-ghosts-scary-stories-from-history/

Learn more about the history of dolls at this museum site:
www.floridamuseum.ufl.edu/sflarch/collections/seminoledoll/dolls/

INDEX